Jim and Debbie Patrick
2018

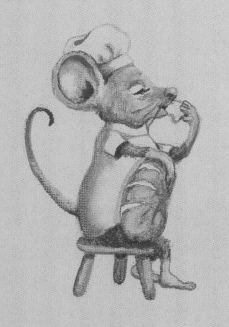

The illustrations by Debbie Patrick are all hand-painted oils on canvas.
Please visit the index at the back to see the original artworks which inspired this book.

www.debbiepatrickart.com

ISBN-13: 978-0-692-14326-1

Printed in China by Global PSD
www.GlobalPSD.com

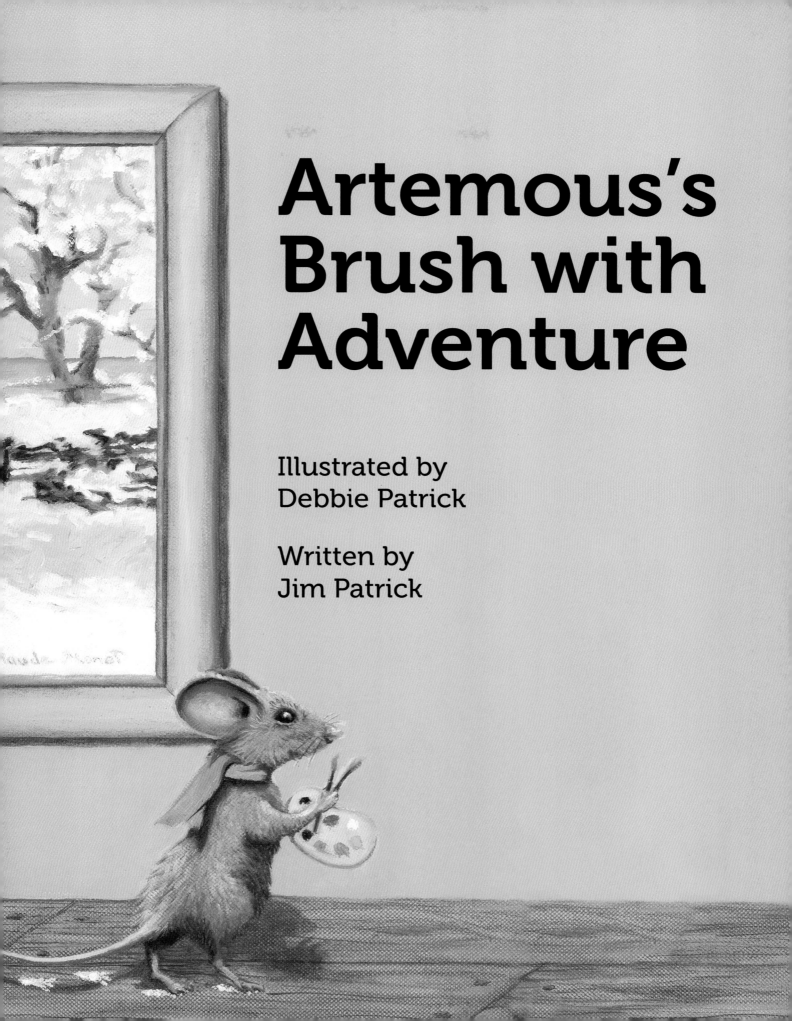

Artemous's Brush with Adventure

Illustrated by
Debbie Patrick

Written by
Jim Patrick

This book is dedicated to artistic mice everywhere
who have stayed too long in the shadows.

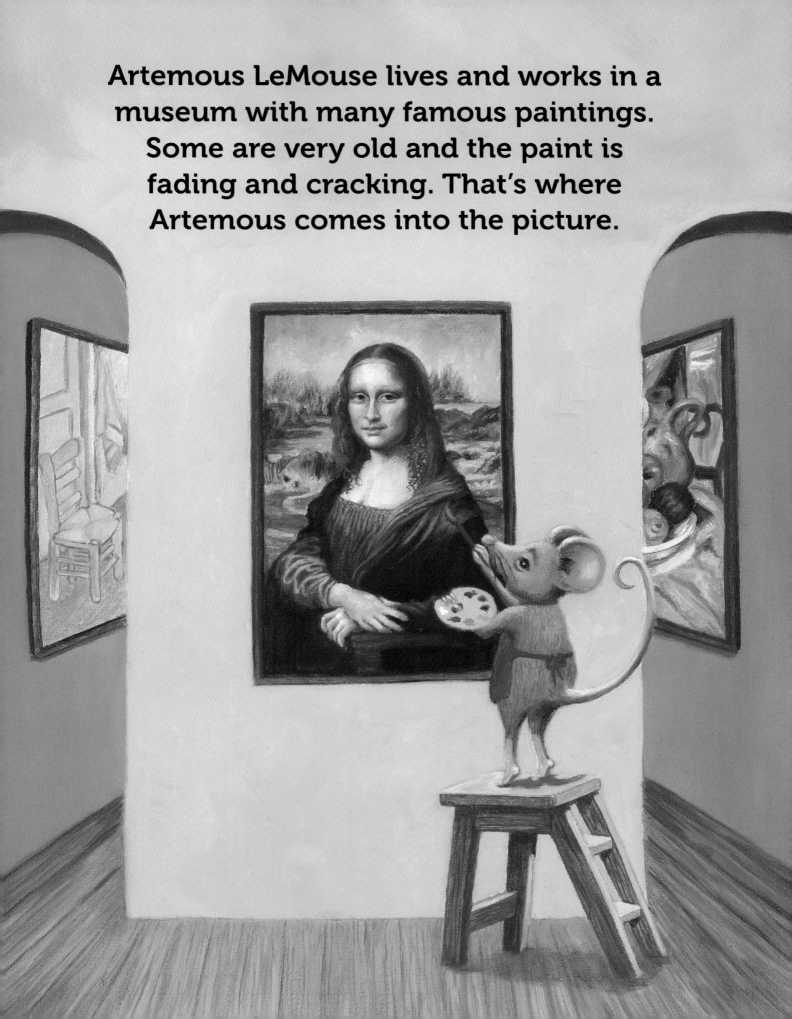

Artemous LeMouse lives and works in a museum with many famous paintings. Some are very old and the paint is fading and cracking. That's where Artemous comes into the picture.

Toulouse LeMouse
1836 - 1851

Artemous is the latest in a long line of
LeMouse art restorers going back more than
300 years. Human years, not mouse years,
which are shorter (just like mice).

Artemous works at night and sleeps during the day, when the museum is filled with art lovers who might be a tad squeamish at seeing a mouse scampering around the museum, lugging his tiny brushes and mouse-sized tubes of paint.

Artemous restores old masterpieces by climbing inside the paintings to do his work. After all, a builder doesn't work on the inside of a house by standing outside it, so why should an art restorer?

He enters the artwork
through a special
mouse hole he paints
on the canvas with
magic paints passed
down from his father
and grandfather.
This mouse hole
lasts only one night.
He must be back in
the museum by dawn.

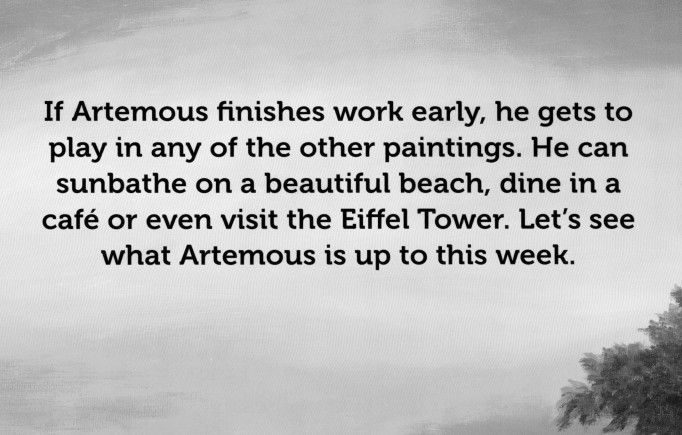

If Artemous finishes work early, he gets to play in any of the other paintings. He can sunbathe on a beautiful beach, dine in a café or even visit the Eiffel Tower. Let's see what Artemous is up to this week.

On Monday, Artemous grabs breakfast, then gets to work touching up the fading plums. He enjoys nibbling on the bread, but has to be careful not to eat too much and have to repaint what he's eaten!

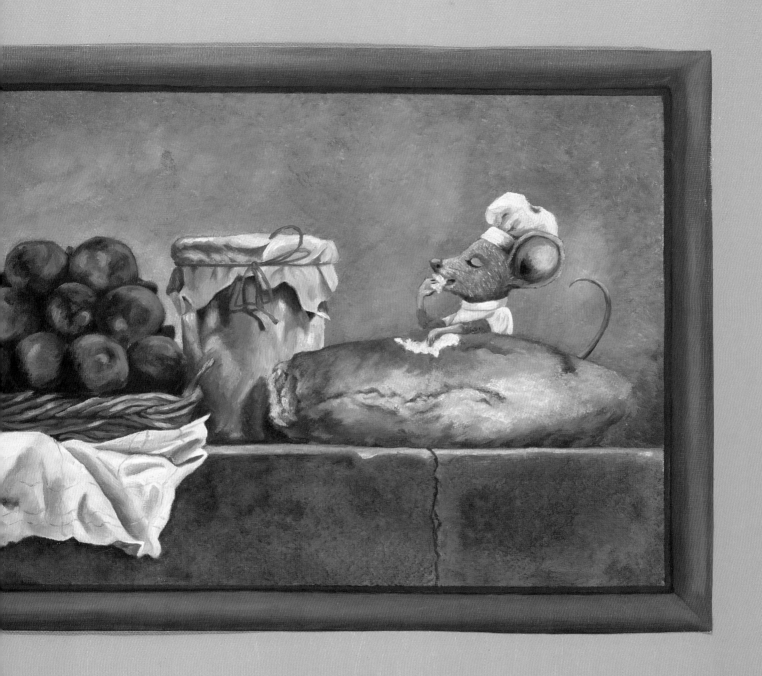

He then heads to the beach and helps children sift through the sand, looking for lost coins, missing rings, and hopefully, better bathing suits! Then he's back at work, restoring the sand that keeps leaking out of the frame.

On Tuesday
Artemous squeezes
in a dance lesson
before work. He
twirls with the
ballerinas, trying
a pirouette in the
curled tail position.

After ballet practice, Artemous works on one of his favorite winter landscapes. He loves to walk in the crunchy snow and feel his whiskers stiffen in the icy wind. But the mischievous black bird refuses to stay where he is painted and constantly flies off the gate, so Artemous keeps painting him back in where he belongs.

On Wednesday, Artemous hides behind his parasol while restoring the paint washed away by constant rain in the masterpiece with the ill-mannered cat. He spends so much time running from this cat with enormous claws that his whiskers droop for days afterwards.

That evening, Artemous strolls to his favorite cafe in all of France and relaxes under a star-filled sky. The waiters enjoy his visits, even though his tips are mostly bits of cheese.

Artemous is also an accomplished artist whose paintings hang in the finest mouse holes in the country. On Thursday, he puts the finishing touches on a tiny portrait of a lady in black.

After cleaning his brushes, Artemous rushes over to the library. He is a great reader and really enjoys the books on the first two shelves (which also happen to be the only ones he can reach).

Artemous loves playing his clarinet
during Thursday night jam sessions
with his three talented musician friends.
Can you spot the dog in the painting,
thumping his tail in time to the music?

Friday morning Artemous craves exercise and fresh air, so he joins the colorfully dressed African women cycling to market. He helps babysit, strapping one of the twins to his back as he pedals his mouse cycle along the dusty road.

In the afternoon, Artemous works on touching up the magnificent collar of the young flute player. He joins his new friend in several lively duets. He's fortunate he has two great ears for music!

On Saturday Artemous helps Princess Marguerite get dressed for her royal portrait. She doesn't care for the gown her mother has chosen, so she's in a crabby mood. Artemous struggles with all the orange satin bows and hopes she will not be too grumpy to smile for her portrait.

That evening, Artemous dresses
in tails and joins the opera lovers.
Once the performance begins, he
perches in the balcony, happily
peering through his mouse-sized
monocle at the spectacle below.

After the long opera, Artemous can't wait to go to bed. Half asleep already, he slips into his nightshirt and wakes up the napping dog, who gruffumbles about being there first, then moves to the end of the bed. Artemous slides under the covers and is soon fast asleep.

On Sunday, Artemous loves to sleep in. Later, when the museum is about to close, he decides to start work a bit early.

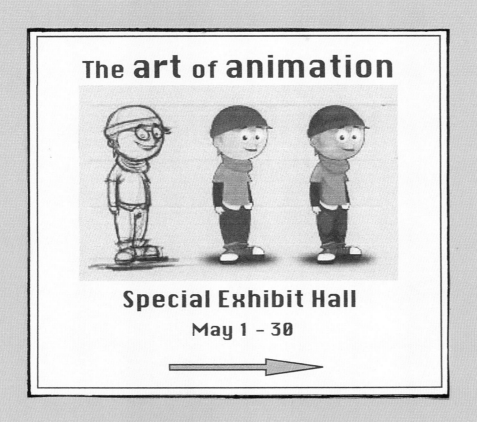

As everyone is leaving the museum, he enters one of the artworks in the Special Exhibits Hall. Suddenly he hears a cry!

MAMA, LOOK!

There's a mouse in this picture!

It is the cry he has always feared.
He has been seen in a painting and now
will surely lose his job. He knows mice
are not welcome in people's homes,
let alone a world class museum!

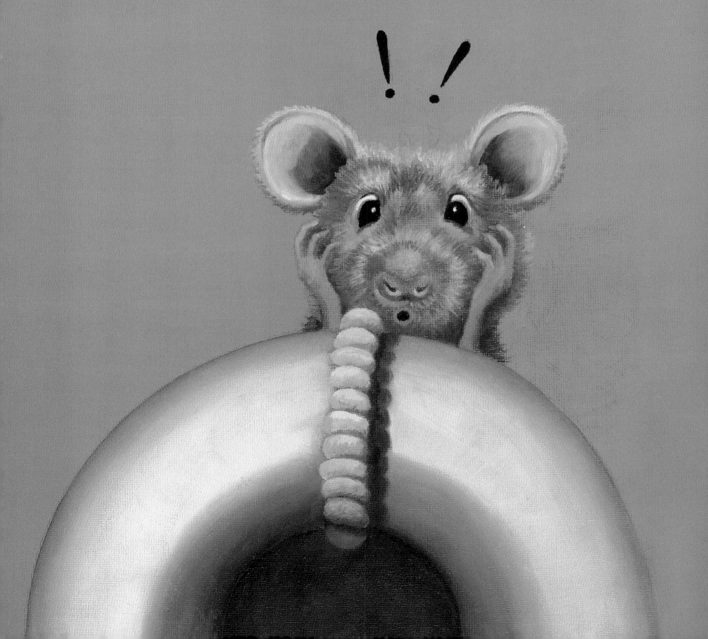

"Of course there's a mouse in the picture," the mom says excitedly. "That's Mickey Mouse from a famous cartoon." The frightened Artemous, who has hidden behind the boat's life preserver, breathes a sigh of relief. His job is safe!

So ends another week in the life of the most famous 6-inch tall art restorer in the world. Next time you visit the museum, see if you can spot him hiding around a corner, waiting for the last art lover to leave so he can get to work.

And once in a great while you may be able to spot a small bit of whisker that he sometimes paints in a corner of an artwork, usually just above the artist's signature. It's his way of letting you know that Artemous LeMouse has been hard at work, restoring another of the world's art treasures.

Mona Lisa
Leonardo Da Vinci
(1452 - 1519)

Sunday Afternoon at the Island of La Grande Jatte
Georges Seurat
(1859 - 1891)

Cape Cod Morning
Edward Hopper
(1882 - 1967)

Still Life with Fruit and Jar of Brown Earthenware
Jean-Baptiste-Simeon Chardin
(1699 - 1779)

Children Playing on the Beach
Mary Cassatt
(1844 - 1926)

Dancers Practicing at the Barre
Edgar Degas
(1834 - 1917)

Café Terrace at Night
Vincent Van Gogh
(1853 - 1890)

The Honorable Mr. Cat
Helen Hyde
(1868 - 1919)

The Bookworm
Carl Spitzweg
(1808 - 1885)

Portrait of Berthe Morisot
Edouard Manet
(1832 - 1883)

Three Musicians
Pablo Picasso
(1881 - 1973)

The Little Dancer
Edgar Degas
(1834 - 1917)

The Magpie
Claude Monet
(1840 - 1926)

Lady Cyclists Joyride
Anthony Bumhira
(1985 -   )

Young Flute Player
Judith Leyster
(1609 - 1660)

L'Infante Marie Marguerite
Diego Velasquez
(1599 - 1660)

At the Opera Ball
Henri de Toulouse-Lautrec
(1864 - 1901)

Master Bedroom
Andrew Wyeth
(1917 - 1966)

Mickey Mouse in Steamboat Willie
Walt Disney
(1901 - 1966)